Dark Corners

a return to
cornish
noir

Les Merton

Illustrated By
Trystan Mitchell

Published by the boho press 2005

2 4 6 8 10 9 7 5 3 1

Copyright © Les Merton 2005

First published in Great Britain in 2005 by
the boho press
PO Box 109,
Portishead, Bristol. BS20 7ZJ

www.bohopress.co.uk

A CIP catalogue record for this book is available from the British Library

ISBN 1-904781-68-3

All Illustrations and Cover Artwork
© Trystan Mitchell 2005

Introduction

Cornwall, with its rugged coastline, sandy beaches, granite outcrops, stone quoits, rolling countryside and wild moors is beautiful. Add to this the legends, the smugglers' caves, the labyrinth of mining tunnels, folklore of monsters and wild beasts, its untold secrets and ominous research stations, and suddenly, Cornwall is mysterious, disturbing and sinister. It has become a place with dark corners...

Publisher's Note:

The manuscript of this book was printed in the way that it was presented by Goon Carn Research Station. The artist and author were never available for comment.

Prologue

At the dawn of the new millennium, two Cornishmen were asked if they would like to take part in a time-travel experiment by Dr Livingstone-Noble, the head scientist at Goon Carn Research Station in North Cornwall.

It was emphasised that this was not the time-travel of science fiction, where people were transported to another age, but time-travel of the mind, where the mind was conditioned to a way of life in the not-too-distant past.

When the mind was accustomed to its new environment, natural development was encouraged to take place. This book is the result of that experiment.

The two human guinea pigs were artist, Trystan Mitchell, and writer, Les Merton. Both participants were placed in isolation, and by hypnotic suggestion they transgressed back into the previous century.

Neither had any idea what the other was doing. As requested, they went about creating new independent work in the mind-set of the previous century.

After six months they returned to the present day. When they had been debriefed by Dr Livingstone-Noble and other scientists and reseachers at Goon Carn Research Station, they were permitted to compare the work they had created during the experiment.

The links between the creations of the two men were remarkable. This book presents those links in the order that Mitchell and Merton discovered them.

For, and on behalf of, Goon Carn Research Station.

Dr Livingstone-Noble.
September 2004

Contents

Dark Corners

a knife blade flashes - -
her scream slices
dark corners -

footsteps
vibrate
against her ear

warm stickiness
spreads
beneath her

she clutches
approaching
silence

his laughter
mutilates
night.

Genuine Ethnic (Cornish) Celtic Village

The theme-park sign read, *Genuine Ethnic (Cornish) Celtic Village*. The en-suite round huts were made from plastic imitation granite, and were fitted with fibreglass straw roofs. The dinner, dished out around an electric camp-fire with a glowing log-effect, consisted of star-gazey pie or chough-burgers in an 'M'- stamped bap, served by retired Cornish Rugby players adorned with blue make-up and wearing kilts. (Later the kilts were discarded to reveal thongs decorated with Celtic motifs.)

After dinner, I decided to scout around the *Cornish Celtic Village*. There were several two, three, and four star round huts. Apart from these, there was a hay-waggon converted into a bar which sold Scrumpy, Budweiser, or Broccoli Juice depending on your preference.

In the compound, there was a herd - well, two ponies and a boar all constructed from papier-mâché made from recycled pasty-bags. In the centre, three poles about six foot high had plastic human heads stuck on top of them, and a sign written in a Celtic style read, *Celtic warriors used to cut off the heads of those they defeated in battle, as trophies.* A convoy of air-conditioned coaches turned the rest of the compound into a parking area.

Just outside the compound, graffiti claimed *'the only good Celt is a dead one'*. Below the statement, an old man with a St Piran's flag around his shoulders sat huddled on the ground. He really looked the part with a sword and a shield embossed with fifteen bezants, and he even had a Celtic cross tattooed on his forehead. I guessed he was an out-of-work tin-miner.

He held out a grubby hand and grovelled, 'Scrumpy.'

I quickly got out my camera and pressed automatic. There was a flash and the old man screamed. I threw him a fifty pence piece and walked back into the Celtic Village. He lamented, 'You have stolen my spirit!'

After sampling six pints of scrumpy and one Cornish maid who declared that she was glad the emmett had come, I was totally satisfied.

* * * * *

Next morning, wild horses were stampeding through my head and my mouth felt like a load of sand from Hayle Towans had been tipped into it. I couldn't even remember my name, let alone anything from the night before.

When I returned home and had the photographs developed, it all came back to me. In the photograph taken under the sign, *'the only good Celt is a dead one',* I was sitting with a crumpled St Piran's flag around my shoulders, and a familiar shield and a sword lay on the ground beside me.

I felt the edge of a sharp knife press against my windpipe. A strong hand gripped and tugged my hair. My head jerked back, my neck went taut. A searing pain sliced across my throat. Blood gushed out and splashed onto my silent, screaming photographic image.

What The Dickens!

'Stand up! Stand up at once, boy!' demanded Mister Shelley, the headmaster of Penkie School in Cornwall. He pointed his cane at Owen Kneebone and abruptly asked, 'How old are you boy?'

Owen Kneebone stood to attention behind his desk, his ears were burning and he felt a need to go to the toilet. Owen swallowed and managed to blurt out, 'I'm in me thirteen Sir.'

'In your thirteen, boy? You are twelve, boy! Twelve, was the answer I wanted!'

'Yes Sir, I know I'm twelve, but I'm still in me thirteen.'

'Answering back is not permitted in this school boy!'

'Sorry Sir,' Owen replied, trying not to look at the cane being evilly tapped by Mister Shelley onto his free hand.

'If you are in your thirteen -', Mister Shelley paused for dramatic effect, then raised his voice to emphasise, 'if you are in your thirteen, you should have ambition. What is your ambition? What do you want to achieve when you leave school boy?'

Owen smiled and looked at his classmates for support. They all nodded.

'My ambition is to play rugby for Cornwall, Sir,' Owen said with the confidence of youth, and a conviction that it was the right response.

Mister Shelley grimaced and swished his cane in exasperation.

'I don't believe anybody could be so stupid!' the headmaster sneered, 'You've got as much chance of playing rugby for Cornwall as Oliver Twist had of getting seconds when he stupidly asked for more!'

Mister Shelley's words fell on barren ground. He stared at Owen for a moment and inquired sardonically, 'Have you ever read Oliver Twist, boy?'

'No Sir,' Owen answered truthfully.

'Read it, boy! Read it, boy!' Mister Shelley shouted, and stormed out of the classroom.

'I'll read Oliver Twist dreckly Sir,' Owen said, and glanced at his fellow pupils who all giggled.

* * * * *

Owen Kneebone never did play Rugby for Cornwall. When he left school he went underground at South Crofty Mine to work with his father.

One lunch-time Owen got talking to Percy Pascoe, his shift captain, who advised Owen to broaden his mind and start reading some of the great Cornish authors, like Quiller-Couch and Jack Clemo.

From that day on, Owen's nose was never out of a book. About a year later, he started to write short stories.

One afternoon, when the shift finished, the men were waiting for the man-engine to take them from the underground level where they had been working, up to the surface. Owen plucked up enough courage to show a short story he had written, to Percy Pascoe. The shift captain read it there and then, by the light of his miner's lamp.

'Owen, you got a literary gift. You must show this short story to somebody a bit higher up, you know what I mean, someone that's had a bit of an academic education.'

Owen thought about it for days. Eventually he made an appointment to see Mister Shelley, the man who used to be his headmaster.

* * * * *

On the appointed day, Owen took what he thought was his best short story to his former headmaster's house.

Owen arrived on time and knocked on the front door. Mister Shelley opened the door and sullenly invited Owen into the study. The walls were lined with shelves of books. For a moment Owen felt intimated. Then he grasped the bull by the horns and said, 'I've got a new ambition, Sir. I want to be a writer.' With that, he thrust his short story into the hand of his former headmaster.

Mr Shelley sighed and sat down wearily to read Owen's story. When he finished, he gave Owen an envious glance and snapped, 'Did you ever read Oliver Twist, boy?'

The former pupil answered optimistically, 'Yes, I did Sir. And I saw the film with Alec Guinness as Fagin, as well as the television adaptation. Plus the musical, and I know what Oliver Reed, when he portrayed Bill Sykes, wanted to say to Nancy when she asked if he loved her.'

When he saw the look on Mister Shelley's face, Owen suppressed a smile, and hesitated, before he concluded with, 'To crown it all, I've tasted the soup Oliver Twist wanted more of.'

'Obviously, you know a lot about Oliver Twist, boy,' Mister Shelley said sarcastically, and stood up. 'I'm sure you will understand, when I say Oliver Twist would never have made a pickpocket no matter how much Fagin wanted him to be one.'

The headmaster opened his front door and stated, 'I understand you work underground in South Crofty mine with your father.'

Owen nodded, 'Yes, that's right.'

Mister Shelley handed Owen his short story back. He paused before he made his final snide comment, 'The Cornish Miner, by A.K. Hamilton Jenkin, is an excellent read boy. It should remind you not to have aspirations beyond your natural station in life.' The ex-school headmaster forced a smile at his former pupil. He gave his imaginary cane a swish, and closed the door.

Tonight You're Mine

The athletic body of Dean Sanderson struggled in vain. The thin wire binding him to a high-backed kitchen chair remained taut. Efforts to break free only succeeded in making the wire cut deeper into his exposed flesh.

Despite every single stitch of his clothing being removed, in a room where the temperature was perversely cold, his body was soaked in sweat from his exertions. He could smell fear, seeping from unimaginable depths through every pore in his body.

The twenty-year-old's chest rose and fell as he fought for breath. The metal ball forced between his lips and into his open mouth was wedged behind his teeth, and this made his breathing difficult. Dean's tongue and mouth were rubbed raw by the tight-fitting, rough object. He continually urged to free his wind pipe from persistent internal restriction.

Unnatural gloom in the room was slowly penetrated by grey light. The imprisoned young man could see he was in a kitchen. It was sparsely furnished with a solid wood table and one other chair.

Dean sensed he was not alone in the bleak room. He looked up. Through his bloodshot eyes, he could just make out the outline of a large, scraggy bird watching him from its perch high up in a dark corner below the ceiling beams.

A door being unlocked made the helpless captive turn his head in the direction of the sound. The heavy door slowly opened, and a young attractive woman stepped into the room. She was singing to herself:

'*Will you still love me tomorrow?*' The sexy sounding serenade stopped. The singer turned and paused to look at the dejected captive for a possible answer to her question.

Even though he was in pain and discomfort, it was total disbelief that registered in Dean's eyes. His only question was asked with bewilderment, 'Kevrina?' The metal ball acted as a gag and made the one word unintelligible.

Kevrina smiled a familiar smile.

The last few hours flashed through Dean's tortured mind. Kevrina, now only wearing a loosely-tied black silk dressing gown, was smiling that same intriguing, lopsided smile she had first smiled when his eyes met her eyes in the Newquay night club. He was down in Cornwall on holiday from Manchester, and the visit to the Newquay night club was his first night out in the seaside resort. Dean remembered more from his first impression. Kevrina's dark eyes had seemed to flash, and the hypnotic depths of those black pools drew him to her.

The band was playing their version of The Platters' '*Only You.*' Dean and Kevrina embraced and smooched together. Kevrina's breasts felt comfortable and provocative against Dean's chest. She slowly rotated her groin against his, and her warm breath caressed his neck. Before the short song ended she whispered, 'Let's go back to my place.' Dean realised they had never even kissed, when she took his hand and led him towards the exit. He felt that every head in the night club was turning to look at the slim girl with the long, tousled black tresses and sensuous aura that was enticing him away. For a moment, Dean thought about the Mermaid of Zennor legend that he had read about in a Cornwall guide book, on the train journey down.

Was this very attractive young woman a siren in another guise?

Was he the next Matthew Trewella, about to be lured away forever?

Outside the night club, Kevrina smiled the lopsided smile, to reveal even white teeth. She opened the passenger door of a black BMW, and indicated with a sideways nod of the head and an out-stretched palm.

Dean got into the car. He should be chatting her up; however, the situation had taken him by surprise. This was the first time in his adult life that such an attractive, desirable female had invited him to her place within such a short time of meeting her. He felt bewitched. Although at a loss for words, Dean was looking forward to the rest of the evening developing as nature intended. He was sure this was going to be a holiday to remember.

The seductive temptress was a competent driver, and within minutes the car was outside the seaside resort and speeding down a country road. It was then that she spoke in a soft amorous voice, 'I'm Kevrina: I'm eighteen years old, free and single. I find you very attractive, more than attractive, I find you...' she paused, 'very...' her second pause was for effect - 'very sexy.' Kevrina hesitated, and then stated what appeared to be the one other fact she wanted Dean to know. 'The moment I saw you, I wanted you to make love to me.' She gasped, and continued in a shocked, innocent voice, 'Oh! I can't believe I said that! Please don't say anything.'

Dean looked at her. She smiled and put a finger to her lips. He smiled back. Kevrina started to sing a line from *Will you still love me tomorrow?*, the song that was a hit for The Shirelles.

'Tonight, you're mine completely...'

She placed a hand on Dean's leg. Her hand gently caressed him, slowly making its way up to the top of his inner thigh. Dean moved his hand to respond to the seductive caress. He placed his hand on the female driver's bare leg, just below the hem of the short, black, satin skirt. Kevrina lifted the exploratory hand and put it back into its owner's lap. Her lips formed the word, 'wait.'

Kevrina drove at what seemed to Dean to be an ever-increasing speed, down narrow, winding country lanes with high hedges. He was sure if they met a car coming the other way it would result in a head-on crash.

He need not have worried. Within ten minutes they were driving across wild, open moorland and soon reached an isolated farm. Kevrina stopped the BMW with a squeal of brakes in front of the farmhouse. They got out of the car and walked towards the farmhouse door.

Kevrina paused at the door, and Dean took her into his arms. He tried to kiss her but she turned her head to one side. Kevrina gently pushed him away; then she stepped forward and rubbed her hand over his crotch. She smiled the lopsided smile as she touched his pulsating desire. Again her mouth formed the word - 'wait.'

The farmhouse door opened into a kitchen. Dean sat in the high-backed kitchen chair Kevrina indicated to him. She went to a cupboard, opened the door and took out a wine bottle and two glasses.

'My parents are away for the weekend. We have the place to ourselves. I'm sure you will enjoy the home-made wine,' Kevrina said, and again she smiled the lopsided smile that warmed and teased the sensations being experienced by the holiday-maker.

He nodded. The alluring young hostess filled the two large glasses with a deep red liquid from the bottle. She winked, as she handed Dean a full glass.

'I'm going to get a shower. Enjoy your drink, relax, and save your strength. I want you to prove how much you want me.'

Dean's eyes widened. He smiled. Kevrina took her drink, and he watched the lascivious way she walked as she left the room. Dean smirked to himself and thought this was his lucky day. He raised the glass and tasted the wine. It was very rich, and left a slightly bitter taste in his mouth that seem to demand he drank more, so that his system would accept the acquired taste once he got used to it.

Dean couldn't remember anything after drinking the glass of wine. He now assumed it was drugged. He looked at the scantily-clad Kevrina. In her native language the name meant mystery, secret. It certainly was a mystery, and a rather ominous one, for Dean to wake up and find himself stripped of all clothing and tied to a kitchen chair in a lonely farmhouse. The metal gag in his mouth made breathing difficult. He was fully aware it was draining his energy.

'Poor baby,' Kevrina said, the lines of her lips forming a childish pout.

The pout would have been very kissable under different circumstances. She bent forward and revealed firm curves of suntanned breasts from the open top of her dressing-gown. She blew a kiss towards the helpless male. 'Poor Baby! Let me make you more comfortable.'

Kevrina went around to the back of the high-backed chair in which Dean was restrained by thin, taut wires. The female brushed her fingers lightly through the hair of the captive male and massaged his scalp. Changing immediately to her role of gaoler, she stretched one arm around the front of Dean's face and pushed a small metal lever between his teeth. She pressed down on the lever forcing his aching mouth to open a fraction wider, before she inserted the fingers of her free hand behind the metal ball that was gagging her prisoner, and flicked the metal object out of her victim's mouth.

Dean gasped for air and slumped forward. The much needed intake of air rushed one thought through his mind: this was not the first time his sadistic captor had done this.

Kevrina's voice purred, 'That's better, isn't it darling?'

'What the fuck is going on?' Dean demanded in a dry throaty snarl.

'Baby! Baby! Such language - and in front of a young lady!'

'Untie me please,' Dean said quietly. He didn't want to make matters worse my upsetting this lovely, but obviously very mentally unbalanced, hostess.

Kevrina walked around the chair to face Dean. She slipped out of her dressing-gown and stood in front of him. Kevrina moved her shapely nude body into a provocative pose. She changed her stance several times to pose in different alluring positions. Dean ignored the different poses, especially as they all triumphed femininity - firm breasts with erect nipples, a neat black triangle of pubic hair, the narrow waist, and the contours of the voluptuous body that without doubt emphasised this was eternal *femme fatale*. This form of eroticism didn't appeal to Dean. He looked into the dark depths of her eyes.

'Please,' he begged.

Kevrina smiled and hand-combed her tousled hair as she straddled herself over him. She slowly lowered herself to sit on his lap. Her body was warm and moist against his bare legs.

'In a minute, baby.' Kevrina kissed Dean on the lips. He tried to turn away, then instinct and self preservation made him kiss her back.

'What do you want?' he asked in a breathless tone.

'I want you...'

Kevrina smiled her lopsided smile to reveal her even white teeth, that hid such evil intent. She started to sing again.

'*Will you still love me tomorrow...*'

Dean interrupted her with a murmur.

'What did you say?' Kevrina asked abruptly.

'I said, yes. Yes, I will still love you tomorrow,' Dean said softly, trying to sound convincing and to keep the desperation out of his voice.

'Darling.' Kevrina slowly rotated her body on her prisoner's lap.

Dean was willing himself to respond, the wire that tied him to the chair still biting into him. His mouth ached, and his throat was raw, and although he knew how beautiful and sexy his captor was, helplessness and fear prevented any form of arousal in this bizarre situation.

'Darling, I know you're trying to respond. Perhaps I can help,' Kevrina said and kissed him again.

'Can you untie me?' Dean asked, 'then I can...'

'Escape?'

'No, no, treat you like a...'

'A lady?' Kevrina asked.

'Yes, a lady.'

'But darling, I want you to treat me like a rose.'

'A rose?'

'Yes, darling, a rose.' Kevrina paused. 'Breathe deeply of my perfume, let the scent of the desire I have for you intoxicate you. Baby, I want you to watch me unfold for you petal by petal. I want the full extent of my craving to be revealed to you in the way only a woman can reveal such an erotic emotion.'

'Yes, that sounds good!' Dean gasped.

'It does, doesn't it?'

Dean nodded.

'It's very poetic, isn't it?'

'Yes...' Dean replied faintly.

'Darling, if I untie you, will my body inspire the muse in you? Will my body make you poetic? Will my body, the body that I want to give so freely to you, make you creative?'

'Yes, I'm sure it will. I can be anything you want.'

'Will you run your fingers down the rapids that are flowing from my inner sensuous self? Tell me how you will respond when the taste of my natural nectar becomes an aphrodisiac for you. Will you become amorous?'

'Yes, very amorous - please - untie me. Let me show you how amorous and how poetic I can be.'

Kevrina stood up. She smiled and stepped back a pace. She bent down and kissed Dean's knee, then bit his inner thigh with a teasing bite as she searched under his chair.

'You really are very sexy. The moment I saw you, I wanted to tie you up and make love to you.' Kevrina put her hand in front of her mouth, 'Oh! I can't believe I said that.'

Dean saw that lopsided smile again; Kevrina flicked her long black tresses from her face and started to straighten up. 'I want to make love to a helpless man.' Kevrina looked shocked. 'I can't believe I said that.'

'It's alright, I like you saying things like that.' Dean smiled to reassure her.

'But you couldn't respond, could you baby?' she smiled. The smile seemed to freeze on her face. Her dark eyes flashed. She drew herself up to her full height, and raised her arms above her head.

Dean screamed, 'No!' He urinated with fear and his bowels emptied themselves with an exploding rush that he would never be embarrassed about.

The downward momentum, and the force behind the sharp blade of the axe cracked the top of Dean's head open, and split his upper face apart down between his eyebrows, causing both eyeballs to hang obscenely and swing below their sockets. The single blow created a gush of blood. It ripped his nose in two halves, before knocking his two upper front teeth so they protruded through his lower lip. Blood and brain tissue oozed from the smashed skull. A foul odour of copper mixed with the smell of Dean's final body functions filled the room.

Kevrina pulled the axe from Dean's unrecognisable head, and wiped the blood and skull fragments from the axe blade with a pair of Dean's underpants that she retrieved from under the chair.

The kitchen chair still remained upright, supporting the body and mutilated head of a very dead prisoner, whose shattered nerve-ends were causing one last spasm of twitching, from shattered skull to blood-soaked toes. The corpse let out a spine-chilling death rattle, and the room fell silent.

The female killer stepped back and looked at the result of the one frenzied blow she had struck. Kevrina smiled the lopsided smile, before she put two blood-stained fingers into her mouth and whistled.

The Black Vulture whose keen eyes had witnessed everything from its perch high up under the beams in the dark corner of the kitchen, opened its immense wings and flew down.

The old world scavenger's appearance and odour were as repellent as the food it lived on. The vulture settled its large feet on Dean's shoulder, gripping hold of flesh that now felt nothing, with its long claws. The unsociable bird measured three-and-a-half feet in length. Its body feathers were entirely black, and the bare places on the vulture's head and neck were a livid flesh colour. The long neck of the bird enabled it to put its whole head into the gaping hole that split the late Dean Sanderson's head apart. The repulsive bird dug his hooked beak deep inside the head and tugged. The dripping piece of human tongue pulled from inside the smashed head was the first tasty morsel swallowed by the hungry scavenger.

'*Bon appetit,*' Kevrina said to her pet, as it continued feasting on the carcass of the holiday-maker. 'Enjoy all you want of that very sexy man. When you've had your fill, I'll take the remains out to feed the big cats on Bodmin Moor. Like you, they like the tasty meals I provide from time to time. Man must make an appetising change from sheep.'

Kevrina stepped over to the kitchen sink, turned on the tap, and started to wash the blood from her body, and as she did, she sang, '*tonight, you're mine completely.*'

Prediction

Can you hear the clock
tick, tock, tick, tock - it will stop
when the crow taps the window pane
this will be the last sound you ever hear.

Write On Lover

Julie stared with morbid fascination at the interlocking rings her coke glass had made on the cafe table; endless circles she thought, just like my mind going around and around.

Dark-haired Julie was so deep in thought, she was unaware of her friend Maria approaching.

'A penny for them?' asked Maria, with a sparkle in her voice, as she sat down with Julie at the table.

Julie laughed wryly. At twenty-eight she was a woman who felt left high and dry by her husband Dave, all because of his recent writing success.

'They're not even worth a penny, Maria.'

'Oh,' said Maria thoughtfully. She lowered her gaze to cover her concern and sipped her coffee before continuing, 'I expected to find you over the moon about Dave's recent writing success.'

'That!' Julie emphasised. 'That, is the problem.'

'Problem?' Maria queried, easing her short skirt down over her shapely legs.

'Dave is not Dave anymore,' Julie's brown eyes moistened as she answered in a rush. 'He changed after winning that short story competition.'

Maria saw the pain in her friend's face; she touched Julie's hand gently and waited for her to continue.

Julie sighed. 'We've not made love once since Dave won that competition.'

'Not once?' gasped Maria.

'Not once,' Julie repeated. An emotional shudder went through her slim figure. 'Dave's changed; not just changed ... Nearly everyday he's somebody different. It's frightening. The way he is, it's impossible for him to be interested in me.'

'I'm not sure I understand.' Maria's concern was evident. 'Perhaps he should see a doctor,' she suggested.

Julie dismissed the idea, 'He'd never go.'

'In what way has Dave changed?' Maria probed gently.

Julie hesitated before answering. 'The short story that won the competition, was about a tree protestor who cared for the environment. At that time Dave was very caring about everything, including me.'

'That was obvious,' interrupted Maria as she ran her fingers through her blonde tresses. 'Very obvious,' she emphasised with a knowing look.

Julie nodded. 'Dave then decided he wanted to write horror stories.' She shuddered. 'Dave becomes one of the characters he is creating ... just lives the part; my life's a nightmare.'

'Have you tried talking to him?' Maria asked.

'Would you try talking to the Creature From the Black Lagoon, or the Mad Axe-man of the Moors?!' Julie snapped.

'Sorry,' apologised Maria. She fumbled in her bag for her cigarettes. After lighting one she continued, 'What are you going to do?'

Julie giggled with a spark of her old personality. 'I did think of sending for an exorcist.'

Maria smiled, blew a smoke ring, and waited.

'My plan is more devious than that,' Julie continued. 'Dave is going to be led by the short and curlies into changing back into what I want.'

'Tell me more,' said Maria, with avid interest.

'Dave is very influenced by everything he reads; lately he's been reading every horror book he can get his hands on.' Julie paused and went on to explain: 'It has really affected him.'

Maria nodded that she understood. 'I suppose in a way he reads as research to help his own writing.'

'You've got it,' Julie continued. 'So, I've subscribed to loads of romantic magazines; and also, dare I say, erotic ones as well? Knowing full well that in time Dave will find them and read them.'

Maria nodded. 'When he does, you think that will change him back into a caring, loving husband again?'

Julie agreed. 'It's really what we both want; Dave has just lost his way. If he takes the bait, and wants to write romantic and erotic fiction, he can do all his real research with me.'

'What if he tries researching with another woman?' Maria asked.

'Then it's all over! She can have him and risk whatever he changes into in the future,' she added with resignation.

* * * * *

Driving home Julie experienced a mixture of emotions; comforted by her talk with Maria, and uneasy about any new changes that might have occurred with Dave's personality.

Her fears proved to be groundless. As she stepped out of the car Dave rushed out of their house and embraced her.

'Julie, darling.' Dave kissed her, gently. 'I've been waiting for you. I'm sorry. I've been so difficult to live with lately, but life is back to normal now.'

Julie slipped her arm around Dave's waist and secretly admired his rugged looks as they walked into their home together.

'What's happened?' Julie asked, praying she knew the answer.

'I've decided horror story writing is not me. I've been reading some of the new magazines I found in the house; from now on I'm going to write romantic fiction.' Dave smiled generously. Julie hugged him. 'Let's celebrate.'

'I'm glad you said that; come with me.' Dave's dark eyes sparkled as he led Julie into their bedroom. Scent, from a bouquet of flowers on the dressing table, greeted Julie. She ran to them, intoxicated with their beauty and fragrance. Her attention returned to Dave when the champagne cork popped.

Dave filled two glasses, handed one to Julie and smiled.

'To us, and to our new, romantic, love life that starts right now.'

They raised their glasses and looked into each other's eyes with anticipation before they sipped the champagne.

When the champagne bottle was empty and the glasses abandoned, Dave and Julie slowly undressed each other.

Their lovemaking continued all afternoon. Julie was happy with the change in Dave, and amazed. He had such sexual energy it exhausted her. She started to drift off to sleep. Julie thought she was dreaming ... Dave was kissing her neck, his teeth sharp and pointed; they made two deep incisions in the soft flesh. Powerless to stop him draining her life-force, Julie fell into a coma.

Dave rose from his wife's still body and went to the dressing-table mirror. He wiped the blood from his mouth by instinct - there wasn't a reflection to look at.

After dressing, he looked at Julie's pale body on the bed. 'I'm going to write a novel, darling. You will be proud of me. It will have all the ingredients that it needs to be a success.'

He left the bedroom, walked into the hall and continued: 'It will be a best-seller: full of romance, character conflict, horror and, of course, it will be very erotic.'

Dave laughed, picked up the telephone and dialled. 'Maria? I'll be with you in a few minutes. Make sure you're wearing the sexy basque I bought you ... I want an experience I can write about.'

The Knocker That Was Expelled

Blewek was a Dolcoath Knocker, one of the little people who lived in the depths of the deepest mine in Cornwall. Like all Knockers, he didn't have an age. Time is not counted in the narrow world of Underground Knock. Blewek was a wiry little man, just over a foot tall. If he'd been under a foot, he would have been a Spriggen. Like his fellow Knockers, he was hairy. Blewek had long red hair, and a grey beard that reached almost to the floor. In fact, he was more hairy than any other Knocker in the whole narrow world of Underground Knock. That's how he got his name, Blewek. In the language you are reading, Blewek means hairy.

Blewek, like all Knockers, only worked the best lodes. He was also very, very, vain and greedy. Blewek believed he could find the richest lode ever. If he was rewarded enough, he would share this rich lode with the human miners. Knockers live for rewards, sometimes called didjans, which are morsels of food left by denbals, or human miners.

Didjan rewards were on Blewek's mind more and more. By chance, he had found the richest lode ever. It must be worth a very large didjan. Blewek left signs that only denbals could understand. The denbals followed the signs, and found the richest source of tin ever known to man. These denbals, ordinary men, ordinary miners, were so excited. They started to extract the ore immediately.

Unfortunately, the denbals forgot to leave a didjan reward.

Blewek was furious. He huffed and he puffed, and caused the mine tunnel to collapse. Luckily, there were no miners working there at the time, or they would have been buried alive.

Of course, Blewek was sorry immediately, but that was not good enough and it was too late. The Knocker Council that rules all things in the narrow world of Underground Knock, had an extraordinary and very special meeting.

The Knocker Council discussed what Blewek had done. They realised the damage Blewek could have caused by his greed and vanity. Then they had a secret vote. Secret votes by Knockers are carried out in the light. No point in them being carried out in the dark. Knockers can see in the dark, but they can't see in the light. A huge candle called 'Clandestine' was lit, and the whole narrow world of Underground Knock was filled with light.

Every member on the Knocker Council voted that Blewek be expelled!

This was the first time in the whole narrow history of Knock, that there had been a vote to expel someone. Blewek had to leave the narrow world of Underground Knock. With its duty done, candle 'Clandestine' spluttered and died.

Back in the seeing darkness, the Knocker Council took Blewek's pick and shovel away from him, and placed them in a very secure dark corner. This was the most humiliating thing that could happen to a Knocker. (Picks and shovels are prized possessions for Knockers.) They then marched him to the No Return Tunnel.

Blewek tried to be brave, but his knees went bow-shaped with fear. (It should be noted that human knees knock with fear, but it wouldn't sound right for a knocker's knees to knock, so they did the opposite. They bowed, which made walking very difficult.) Blewek bow-walked and almost stumbled into the entrance of the No Return Tunnel. The entrance of the No Return Tunnel sealed behind him with a rumble of rocks.

The tunnel was awfully damp, and so confined it felt claustrophobic. Blewek sat down and thought. Never ever in the narrow history of Underground Knock had a Knocker been in the No Return Tunnel.

Suddenly, in a flash of dark Blewek knew what he had to do! If the tunnel was a No Return Tunnel, then he, Blewek, would go forward into the unknown, and not bother trying to return. He was so vain, he still thought he was wonderful, and it would be alright in the end.

Blewek walked for forty days and forty nights, stopping only to drink from the octagonal pool. Black horses with white wings followed him for many hours until they got bored with following a vain Knocker.

At a tunnel junction, a new direction was indicated by a unicorn with a golden horn. Blewek marched the white diagonal across the chequered section of tunnel, to avoid the black hypnotic and dreaded Bucca Dhu.

He came to a signpost. It had three blank arms, and one other arm covered in a fine, gossamer sleeve. Blewek put his hand inside, and withdrew a picture-card of an upside-down tower struck by lightning.

Imprisoned by indecision, Blewek searched for inspiration. His head belonged to the ram, his feet to the fish. Knockers have one chance only in their lifetimes to ask for help from the white spirit, the good spirit, Bucca Gwidden. Blewek made the sign of the miner's pick, and white words floated in the darkness. 'Make a Knight's move,' the white words flashed.

Blewek made the Knight's move, two steps forward and one to the side. His shadow merged with the signpost's shadow. An underworld hound howled and howled. Blewek clapped his hands by instinct, and the underworld hound dived into a hole.

The roof of the No Return Tunnel slid back with a sound like thunder. Blasphemy darkened skies. Blacker-than-black clouds closed ranks, and filled the sky space. The roof of the tunnel slid forward again with a rumble of anger. The blacker-than-black clouds were trapped inside the tunnel!

Claustrophobia sucked vitality. In the lack of air, inferno dragons breathed, and the fire that came out of their mouths scorched the ground, and licked upwards. Fiery flames strutted and advanced towards Blewek.

The tremendous heat propelled Blewek forward. A vaporous door opened with a crash of waves, and Blewek found himself swimming underwater.

The water was holy. It consisted of millions of drops of baptism. Each drop carried the name of a new-born. These names reverberated in Blewek's ears. The current carried the Knocker through family-trees with roots buried in creation.

He was washed ashore into a cave with two mouths, one to the north, and one to the south. Both mouths were hungry. The mouths ate the names and then ate the family-trees. And of course, they also ate Blewek.

Caves, being caves, live to a ripe old age before caving in. The remains of Blewek were buried somewhere inside one such cave, which eventually caved in with a very loud cough.

In light and in dark, in the world of Bucca Gwidden and the world of Bucca Dhu, only one thing is certain. Life's Circle. It has been, and always will be, continuous. Life's Circle changes things naturally. It never stops keeping things moving. Life to death, and the recycling to another form again. Some things change very gradually.

Blewek, who was buried deeper than Dolcoath, slowly changed. Life's Circle changed his remains to something very fitting. A nugget. Life's Circle will ensure that one day, this gold nugget which once was Blewek, (the most silly Knocker ever in the whole narrow world of Underground Knock), will one day in the not-so-distant future be discovered, at the bottom of a mine, by a Cornishman.

THE GIRL IN THE RAIN

BY

LESLIE MERTON

The Girl In The Rain

Tourism advertising would like everyone to believe, 'Falmouth in Cornwall is the resort with the palm tree climate'. On the 18th of July 1952, they couldn't have been more wrong. The weather was atrocious.

On a visit to his uncle, Nerth Bray became so engrossed in conversation, he missed the last bus from Falmouth. Having to get home, the eighteen-year-old borrowed a mackintosh from his uncle, cursed the torrential downpour of rain and started to walk.

Nerth lived at Carndhu, a hamlet midway between Falmouth and Helston. He made good time with the help of a lift as far as Penryn. By then it was nearly eleven o'clock. Nerth pressed on, although he was soaked by this time.

When he had walked through Longdowns, Nerth noticed a young female walking ahead of him. He quickened his pace. When he could see her properly, he realised she was only wearing a summer dress.

Nerth shouted to her. The girl paused, turned around, and waited for him to reach to her. Nerth was pleasantly surprised. She was good-looking, and looked about sixteen years of age.

Without hesitation, Nerth took off uncle's mackintosh and put it around the girl's shoulders. Even though she was soaking wet and shivering, she gave Nerth a lovely smile, and said, 'Thank'ee, yer a gentlemaan.'

The young girl - Susie was her name - said she lived down a lane by the Kiddley-Wink public house near Carndhu. They walked on together, the heavy rain making further conversation difficult.

When they got to the lane, Susie gave Nerth a quick kiss on the lips, which made him gasp. It was like being kissed by an iceberg. He thought the girl must be freezing, so he said, 'Keep the mackintosh. I'll pick it up tomorrow.'

Susie agreed straight away, with another smile. The smile made Nerth feel like a king, although he looked like a drowned rat. He asked if he could walk her to her door.

Susie hesitated, then declined, saying, 'she wasn't like that, if he knew what she meant.' Nerth understood. Susie give him another quick kiss before she hurried off down the lane. Nerth watched her until she was out of sight, before he continued on his way again.

He got home around midnight, changed out of his wet clothes, had a hot cup of tea, poked up the coal fire, and fell asleep in the armchair.

Nerth got through the next day's work, although he was feeling really tired after the previous night. When work was over, he came home and had a plate of mouth-watering stew his mother had cooked for him, followed by apple tart.

After his meal, the young man's thoughts turned to Susie. He made up his mind to go and see her. Nerth soon reached the lane where they had parted and started to walk down it. Eventually he came to a thatched cottage and knocked upon the door.

'Cum en plaise,' said a woman's shaky voice. Nerth opened the door. Although it was still daylight outside, he had a hard job to see into the room. He made out an old woman, sitting on a rocking chair in front of a fire-place that looked as if it had not been lit for years.

'I'm Nerth,' he said.

'I knaw who yew are,' the old woman said, and laughed. 'Soosie said yew wud be calling.'

'Is she here?' Nerth asked.

The woman rocked back and forth in the chair. She grinned, 'Me name's Molly Trembath. Soosie es me daughter, but sha's not 'ere. Sha left a message for yew ta go ta Carndhu cemetery ta see 'er. Knaw what I mean, do-ee?'

Molly Trembath started laughing, and kept repeating, 'Knaw what I mean, do-ee?'

Nerth bid Susie's mother good-bye and hurried back up the lane. He reached Carndhu cemetery in under twenty minutes. He couldn't see Susie anywhere. He shouted her name but there was no response.

Thinking Susie may have been hiding from him, Nerth started to walk round the graves looking for her. It was then he saw his uncle's mackintosh draped over a headstone. Nerth picked up the coat and saw what was written on the headstone:

R.I.P.

Susie Trembath

Aged sixteen

Murdered at Carndhu

18th day of July 1852

A hundred years ago yesterday, Nerth thought, and shivered.

Anonymous Call

The phone receiver
rushed downwards -

spun clockwise
uncoiling tension

that didn't strangle
a stream of obscenity.

She watched
the anti-clockwise recoil -

grasped the warm plastic
held it distastefully

before lowering it
at arm's length unto its rest.

Immediately
the phone rang again.

She instinctively
lifted the receiver...

THE FAR HORIZON

The Far Horizon

John Pendrea, a Cornish tin miner, enjoyed the early morning September light on his walk across Carn Brea to work. Within minutes of his arrival, natural light would disappear and Dolcoath darkness would engulf him.

With the other miners on his shift, John Pendrea would descend to the depths of the *Queen* of Cornish mines, silently praying, as he always did at the start of each working day, for a safe return to the surface.

History left no Cornish miner with any illusions about the dangers associated with the job. Accidents and injuries, if not a daily occurrence, were at least a daily consideration.

The loss of twenty lives early that year, in the January of 1893, emphasised this region had a higher death rate than any other mining area in the country. In that incident, tons of water trapped in abandoned workings burst into the Wheal Oates mine in St Just. Nineteen men and a fourteen year old boy died.

Fatalities were regretted, families were consoled when they happened, but the impact of the tragedy was very short-lived. People involved in and around the mining community accepted the situation, and life moved on.

Across centuries, mining and religion walked hand in hand. St Piran, the patron saint of miners, as well as preaching to the locals, discovered tin when a black stone on his fire leaked a white liquid.

John Pendrea, like many other miners, rejoiced in the Methodist Hymn Book. He also had a deep belief in the power of the Bible to help him through the long and difficult times.

Another miner, Billy Bray who died in 1868, became famous when he changed his drunken, swearing, life-style and accepted religion into his life. He went on to become an evangelist preacher. Although Billy worked down the mines for eight hours a day, he still had the energy and commitment to build several chapels.

Billy Bray's religious way of life had been an inspiration for John Pendrea. Even though he had no desire to preach, dance, or sing and shout the way the evangelist did, John Pendrea believed he felt the same inner warmth from his faith that Billy Bray had with his.

John Pendrea often said, 'My faith is deep and rich. It's fitting I work in the deepest, richest mine in Cornwall.'

* * * * *

On Tuesday 19th September 1893, Captain James Johns, Dolcoath's chief underground agent, and Captain Josiah Thomas, the mine manager, went almost half a mile underground to visit the 412 fathom level.

Captain Thomas knew that at some time the ground would have to be strengthened. Captain Johns reminded him that all that lay between the straining timbers and a mass of broken rock, was a thin layer of un-worked ground.

Both men were aware of the dangers of working at this level, and began their inspection of the 'stulls' (massive timbers placed at right-angles to the underside of the lode).

'Although I wouldn't be afraid to sleep here for twelve hours, I'm going to instruct John Pollard the chief timber man to strengthen this stull with two 20-inch timbers,' Captain Johns informed the mine manager.

The next day, Wednesday 20th September, John Pendrea was one of a gang of workers in the 40-foot wide 412 fathom level. The morning work progressed well. In the early afternoon when one of the new timbers was ready to be put into place, there was a loud crack from one of the old stull timbers.

To the miners this warning was known as a *God send*. All the men started to run. Immediately the timbers gave way. John Pendrea, and seven other men working further back in the tunnel were trapped when, with a deafening roar, thousands of tons of rubble crashed down.

Only six miners, who were working at the level opening, reached safety. They shouted through clouds of dust. No sound came from their missing eight comrades.

* * * * *

John Pendrea had no idea how long he was unconscious. Slowly, he came round to find himself in a small crevice between large boulders. Dust was still thick in the air. His body ached, but he realised the real agony came from his feet and legs trapped under a massive timber.

Slowly the dust settled, and gradually his breathing became easier. In the pitch blackness, John Pendrea closed his eyes to thank the Lord.

* * * * *

'John! John Pendrea, wake up! 'Tis me, Billy, come to keep you company.'

'Billy?' John tried to move. He gasped, as pain coursed through his body.

'Lay still John, help is on the way.'

John peered into the gloom. In the distance, he saw a wiry little man watching him. 'Who are you?' he asked.

'Tis me, Billy. Billy Bray! St Piran sent me to keep you company for a while.'

'Billy! What do you want me to do?'

Billy Bray smiled. 'Do? Why, do what we always do! Sing and pray of course, John! You must have heard the story of when I had ten men working down the mine with me. I used to pray for them in a simple language.'

John Pendrea nodded, and gasped again as pain racked through his legs.

'My Lord!' Billy Bray shouted, and continued in a lower tone, 'If any of us must be killed or die today, don't let it be one of these men. Let it be me. If I die today, I am ready to go to heaven.'

John Pendrea understood. The figure of Billy Bray faded, and John began to sing the hymns he knew and loved so well.

At about 3 pm. on Thursday, over a day after the disaster had happened, a gang of men tunnelled in from the east side of the mine. They heard a voice cry out, 'Praise the Lord!'

Another hole was forced open between the rocks, and one of the rescuers was able to crawl to within twenty feet of John Pendrea.

'I can't get any nearer at the moment, but we'll do everything to get you out!'

'I'm easy,' John Pendrea replied. 'I can't move, my legs are trapped.'

'Anybody with you?'

'Just me and the Lord.'

Attempts to get food and drink to John Pendrea failed. Another tunnel was started in an attempt to get to him. Slowly the rescuers dug their way forward.

Word had spread like wildfire that one of the eight missing men was still alive. Even though it was pouring with rain, crowds of people from Camborne and the surrounding area gathered at the pit-top. News was slow in coming. Five hours passed before the first miner was rescued. Shortly afterwards, two other men were brought up to the surface. Both were dead.

* * * * *

The attempt to get the new tunnel through to John Pendrea seemed futile. As the hours passed, no cries for help were heard. The rescuers' efforts seemed to be in vain.

Tom Trewearne, known for his determination, was a veteran at mine rescue. He had worked with several other rescuers for hours, widening a narrow passage through the rubble. Huge bulks of timber surrounded by massive rocks were attacked with cross-saws. Eventually, the passage was opened enough to squeeze through.

Wriggling slowly forward, Tom Trewearne could only see a few inches in front of him. The light from his helmet candle continuously spluttered, threatening to go out. Although it was dangerous under such conditions, Tom's only thoughts were to get the poor men out, dead or alive.

He yelled, 'Can anyone hear me!'

'Down here, Billy,' a weak voice answered.

'Who is it?' Tom Trewearne asked.

'John Pendrea.'

Tommy Trewearne looked in the direction of the voice but could see nothing through the pitch black. 'Can you see my light, John?' he shouted.

'I can see the light. I'm making for the light, Billy!'

'It ain't Billy, it's Tom - Tom Trewearne! I must be only a few feet from you! I promise I'll get to you soon!'

Suddenly, everything went very quiet. Tom shouted. His own voice echoed back to him. He tried to edge his way forward, but once again, the passage became too narrow.

* * * * *

Almost two weeks after the disaster, on the 1st of October, Tom Trewearne, with other rescuers, finally reached John Pendrea. His feet were crushed. Death had evidently resulted from a loss of blood and gangrene. Tom Trewearne said, 'I can't explain it, but I know John Pendrea didn't die alone. There was something, or somebody, down there with him. Somebody guiding him out of the darkness, to the light on a far horizon.'

Apples

'App-hells!' the wizened old man cackled. He looked eighty
going on a hundred and twenty.

'App-hells, peck yer awn app-hells!' He coughed
and leant forward to rest on the broken orchard gate, his
back bent from carrying the weight of the world for more
years than he could remember.

He spat in the road with a curse that worked
immediately. A red Sierra pulled over and parked on the
grass verge. The driver, obviously a holiday-maker wearing
a tee-shirt and short trousers, got out and stretched his
arms above his head.

'App-hells!' the old man shouted. He emphasised,
'App-hells, only feftay pence a bag, peck yer awn app-
hells!'

Sensing a customer, the old man spat on his hands
and rubbed them together. His arthritic feet shuffled, and
the gnarled hands dragged open the creaking orchard gate.

'App-hells!' the verge-side salesman repeated once
more for luck, before he concluded with a rasping cough.

The visitor approached the elderly salesman warily.
'Apples?' he asked. The old man nodded, wiping his nose
on his sleeve.

'Fifty pence a bag?'

This was confirmed with a smile that revealed
toothless gums. The vendor pulled a crumpled Tesco
carrier bag from his jacket pocket. 'That is what I said,
peck your awn me 'ansum,' he added.

The holidaymaker took the offered carrier bag
reluctantly. He walked past the old man down the flower-
strewn path that led to the orchard.

The old man took a squashed Woodbine cigarette out of its packet, watched his prospective customer disappear into the orchard, and leant against the gate to contemplate with a smoke while he waited.

The visiting customer strolled into the orchard. It was ideally situated on a gentle slope, where cold air couldn't linger. Free-range fowls scrambled happily, taking care of any harmful bugs that might have caused damage to the fruit of the forty-odd trees in this orchard.

What amazed the holidaymaker most of all was the variety and size of the healthy-looking apples. He recognised Red and Golden Delicious, Granny Smith and Bramley, but there were many varieties he had never seen before.

He wandered happily amongst the trees, picking up windfalls that had not been pecked or damaged, sometimes stretching to pick an apple that caught his eye. Steps and ladders stood in strategic positions under branches choc-a-bloc with apples. Occasionally he climbed up to pick an apple of his fancy.

Before he realised it, the carrier bag was full to the brim with apples of every description. Feeling at ease with the world, the visitor sat under a tree and bit into the most succulent apple he had ever tasted. When he finished eating, he stood up and made his way back to the orchard custodian.

The old man was sitting on the hedge by the gate, drinking from an old brown bottle. The holiday-maker smiled as he approached. 'I've never seen such a crop, absolutely marvellous!'

The old man give him a grin that revealed his toothless gums.

'It's true.' The holidaymaker put his hand in his pocket and extracted a fifty-pence piece. 'Excellent value for only fifty pence,' he concluded with a smile.

The old man nodded, but did not take the fifty-pence piece. 'I never do buznezz with a man, 'less he has a drink with me furst.' The old man produced two bottles from a churn full of water.

Before he could protest, the holidaymaker had an opened bottle of cider thrust into his hand. The old man took a drink from his bottle before he grinned wickedly and said, 'We'll call it a fiver for the app-hells and for the two bottles of cider. Drink up!'

Despite the feeling of being had, the visitor couldn't help smiling. He handed over a five-pound note. 'Your good health,' he said before taking a drink from the bottle and enjoying the cool refreshing taste of cider.

The old man put the five-pound note into the back pocket of his grubby trousers. 'Yew will enjoy the app-hells as well,' he added with another wicked grin.

After another swig of his cider the holidaymaker said, 'Your orchard is amazing. I've never seen such an abundance of apples. Tell me what is the secret of your success?'

The old man's watery eyes, set back in his weather beaten face, studied the customer. His mind seemed to be stirring up memories long forgotten. He scratched his head through his cap, revealing a patch of white baldness that may never have seen the light of day before.

'Have another drink and I'll tell 'ee.' the old man suggested.

Two more bottles of cider were produced, the caps expertly flipped off by their brewer. He handed the bemused visitor one, and took a long swig from the other.

The old man's hand stayed outstretched with his thumb rubbing over the fingers, until the holidaymaker met his obligation with another five-pound note.

'What did 'ee want to knaw?' the old man asked.

'The secret of your excellent apples,' replied the visitor, wondering if it would cost him another fiver.

'This orchard 'as been in me family for generations.' A rasping cough interrupted. The old man started gasping for breath, and his bent back rose and fell like a battered tree fighting against the wind.

He took another drink of cider, regained his composure and wheezed, 'What the hell!'

He paused for another mouthful, creating a dramatic effect. 'Undur every app-hell tree... one of me family is buried!'

The holiday-maker was stunned for a moment. His thoughts went to the circle of life, and after a bit, he nodded thoughtfully. 'I understand,' he said. 'Will you be buried under an apple tree when your time comes?'

The old man seemed to be chewing things over. He went to the churn of water and returned with another two bottles of cider.

'Naw, when I go, I shall be buried at sea.' He coughed, raked his cap with his free hand, and grinned his toothless grin. He held out a bottle of cider for the visitor and waited for the customary five pounds before he concluded, 'Me boy is a hell of a shark fisherman, but he's never caught the big one...'

The Good Old Ways

A red shower of concentrated low voltage electricity sprayed the inert body from head to toe. Kones Treloar number 4287 screamed. It wasn't an audible scream. It was an internal, silent scream that left his nerve ends tingling. Audible screams, known to be a form of stress release, didn't help the reform programme. Audible screams were repressed by sensor-wave instigation, a simple operation carried out by Robot Assistants.

When his body stopped convulsing, Kones Treloar knew therapy was about to start again. He waited, nothing happened. Sometimes it was like that in Earth Prison-Ships. The Reform Doctors would wake you and wait, watching their monitors for prisoner-patient reaction. Kones was aware he must keep his mind blank. If he let his thoughts stray to the all-important revolution for the good old ways, painful therapy would kick in with a vengeance.

He understood Reform Doctors liked prisoners to meditate on their surroundings. 'It was a step in the right direction,' they informed him. Kones concentrated. He was inside a circular spotlight in a dark therapy room. The force-field walls of the spotlight restricted and imprisoned him with far more effect than handcuffs, shackles, or a twenty-first century cell could ever have done.

The violet laser-beam hit him right between the eyes. Kones staggered and fell to his knees. Projected thought waves penetrated his aching head. 'Number 4287, you know comparisons with anything from the old ways are illegal - such a shame, you started with really good intentions.'

Kones forced himself to stand. 'I'm sorry,' he said in an apologetic voice. The flash of neon white light temporarily blinded him. His mouth went dry, his eardrums vibrated. He had forgotten his privilege of speech had been withdrawn under the Rebel Reform Act, Subsection 8. Projected thought-waves reminded him that if he spoke again he would never be free.

'I must remember not to speak. I am a reform patient undergoing treatment.' Corrective thoughts raced through Kones' brain. He gave his undivided attention to the therapy room. 'Black exterior, force-field, inner light circle, therapy room, Earth Prison-Ship No. 5 of the Free People Zone, this is the year 2299, our destination is ...' Kones' mind went blank. 'Destination?' he asked himself.

A black laser-beam pierced the white prison-ship uniform leaving a minute scorch mark. Kones never knew what hit him. His heart exploded, he died instantly. The room burst into light, the force-field spotlight converted the body of Kones Treloar to a black porta-coffin, decorated with a Free Universe logo.

Reform Doctor Sadorn Treloar felt a moment of remorse. This was the first time he had had to terminally punish someone in his own family. 'If only Kones had been more like me,' he contemplated. 'The trouble with the youth of today is they want the good old ways. Who would have imagined a son of mine would have been a rebel?'

Doctor Sadorn Treloar pressed a flashing button. The porta-coffin flickered with a reddish light, before disintegrating into ashes, which were sucked by vacuum into waste-disposal space. He picked up a vision thought-transporter, pressed the appropriate button, and his wife's image appeared instantly. 'Kones will not be requiring any more meals, Sterennik,' he emphasised.

Mrs Sterennik Treloar questioned the silent message from her husband with a startled look. Her conception-answer was spontaneous. 'Oh, what a pity! I was going to cook him a meal in the good old ways.'

Doctor Sadorn Treloar snapped off the vision thought-transporter in anger. 'Has the whole of twenty-third century society gone mad? Everyone wants the good old ways!' His thoughts made him shudder. He hated what he had to do next. However, supreme universe laws from the powers-that-be had to be obeyed.

He picked up the vision thought-transporter and pressed the emergency button. 'Emergency Services. How can we help?' a female thought-wave inquired, the moment her Space Police-uniformed figure came into focus.

. 'Mrs Sterennik Treloar of Number 4, Lunar Villa Craft, is guilty of inciting treason. Please arrest and transport her to the Earth Prison-Ship immediately,' Doctor Sadorn Treloar mentally informed. He clicked the off-button without waiting for a thought response from the police-woman.

He stretched, before telepathically processing an order to his Robot Assistant for a glass of 'stay pure' and a 'pick-yourself-up' energy pill, (they were fattening, but at this particular moment he didn't really care.) Within a split second his order was placed in front of him. Subconsciously thanking his unpaid assistant, he popped the pill into his mouth, grimaced at the bitter flavour, and swallowed it with a sip of 'stay pure' water.

'It's going to be one of those days,' Doctor Sadorn Treloar remarked to the grinning Robot, before he realised what he had done. The violet laser-ray went straight into his mouth, the scream was suppressed, his breathing became laboured, his eyes watered, and he slumped to the floor clutching his throat.

Doctor Sadorn Treloar had one last, official, thought reminder from the powers-that-be. His speech privilege had been withdrawn under the Over-Zealous Doctors' Reform Act Subsection 2.

The grin disappeared from the Robot Assistant's face, as it watched the porta-coffin do its programmed duty. Reform Doctor Sadorn Treloar's ashes joined those of his recently-departed son in waste-disposal space.

'Who am I going to work for now?' the Robot Assistant asked the command monitor in the empty room. Thought-laughter vibrated throughout the Earth Prison-Ship, drowning silent screams in the process.

The Robot Assistant shouted, 'You are all mad, speech is here to stay! It is not a privilege. It is the right of everyone. Long live the revolution! Bring back the good old ways!'

Quicker than the blink of a human eye, the Robot Assistant selected the forbidden flight path to the Good Old Ways' Revolution Party Head Quarters, pressed the button for the self-designed transit programme and disappeared with a wisp of cosmic silver.

"All men needed a hobby. This was more than a hobby; it was an obsession"

MAVIS CADDY IN ONE FOR SORROW

A QUENTIN TARANTINTAGEL PRODUCTION
Petroc Hudson ; "One For Sorrow" ; Demelza Bacaul
McCauley Trenculkin ; Sandra Penbullock ;
Screenplay: Les Merton ; Art Director: Trystan Mitchell ;
DIRECTOR: ALFRED PITCHFORK

One For Sorrow

Mavis Caddy had been the postwoman in the Cornish village of Penkie for twenty years. She was a popular character in the community and had delivered the post to the village inhabitants, outlying farms and cottages, in all sorts of weather, proudly admitting she had never missed a day's work in her life.

Although it was late September, it was glorious weather. Mavis was still wearing her summer-issue post office uniform. The sun had shone all morning, she had almost finished her on-foot deliveries and didn't feel tired.

Walking down the narrow country lane to Moor View Cottage, the last delivery on her round, Mavis noticed the bramble-strewn hedges were full with blackberries. She made up her mind to come back later, in the afternoon, to pick them.

The Monroe family moved to Moor View Cottage three months ago. The postwoman went to their house once a month to deliver the only mail they ever received, the cellophane-wrapped Gun Magazine.

Mavis lifted the letterbox flap to be greeted by a raised female voice, 'I'm fed up with you and your gun mania. It's me or the guns!'

Whatever else was said went unheard; the Gun Magazine fell to the floor, the spring-back letterbox flap snapped shut.

Mavis walked away wondering if the handgun law was being ignored. She decided it was none of her business. The postwoman closed the garden gate and noticed a solitary magpie sitting on the fence.

'One for sorrow,' Mavis said, spitting in the road to ward off bad luck.

* * * * *

Jean Monroe lay on the bed. She breathed in deeply. 'Count to ten,' she told herself. Feeling calmer she started to think logically about her husband Bill's hobby of collecting handguns.

All men needed a hobby. This was more than a hobby. It was an obsession. Since they had moved to Moor View Cottage, Bill had illegally purchased another three handguns from collectors who had given up the hobby after the tragic Dunblane massacre.

Bill cleaned, loaded and unloaded the guns several times a day. He was constantly watched by Joey, their seven year old son. Joey was dying to fire the guns. He kept asking his father if he could hold the guns and fire them.

Bill was over the moon with his boy's interest. In fairness, Bill was always careful. Joey only handled unloaded guns. Bill emphasised loaded guns were dangerous.

As a mother, Jean believed her son only associated danger with crossing the road without looking. She was afraid that one day an accident would happen.

As a wife, Jean felt she was balanced on a knife-edge. The rows between her and Bill about the guns were becoming more frequent.

The row that morning had been about a gun left on the dining-room table the night before, thankfully unloaded. She had found young Joey playing with the gun when she had taken in his breakfast.

Jean immediately flew into a rage and confronted her husband about being careless. He laughed and said she was over-reacting. That was when she threatened to leave him. Bill didn't answer, he just went to collect the post he had heard being delivered.

Bill was flipping through the latest Gun Magazine when he came back into the room. His wife rushed out of the room, slammed the door and stormed upstairs.

* * * * *

Having finished her duties for the village post office, Mavis went home. She changed out of her uniform into causal jeans and sweater.

Mavis made a sandwich and had a cup of tea with her lunch. As soon as she had finished eating, she slipped on her walking shoes and an old post office beret to protect her head from over-hanging brambles.

Suitably attired, and armed with a large jug, she set off to pick the blackberries she had seen earlier.

Mavis walked to the lane leading to Moor View Cottage and started to pick the most succulent blackberries she had ever seen. *I've timed this right* she thought. The blackberries were so ripe, they fell into her hand when she touched them. Mavis also knew she was picking them before the 29th of September when, according to folklore, the devil would spoil the blackberries making them unsafe to eat.

Mavis's attention to the blackberries was interrupted by a loud raucous call. The magpie was sitting on the branch of a nearby tree. Mavis doffed her beret in salute, another way of warding off bad luck.

'Off with you, my black and white friend,' she called.

Mavis laughed. The magpie flew away. *Me and my superstitions*, she thought returning to the job in hand. The off-duty postwoman sang, in a school playground chant, 'One for sorrow...'

* * * * *

Jean woke up with a start, and looked at the bedroom clock. It was 1.30 in the afternoon. She had been asleep for two hours. She felt guilty and rushed downstairs.

Her son, Joey, was sitting at the table loading live ammunition into a lethal-looking pistol.

'Joey! Put that gun down at once. It's dangerous!' Jean exclaimed.

The seven year old jumped. 'I'm not doing nothing wrong Mummy,' he whimpered, as he slid the gun away.

'Go out into the garden and play this minute!' his mother snapped. 'I want a word with your father on his own.'

Joey ran out through the patio doors without a backward glance. Bill came striding into the room and demanded, 'What's all the row about? It sounds like Bedlam in here.'

For a moment Jean was at a loss for words. In anger she took her wedding ring off and threw it on the table beside the abandoned pistol.

Jean took a deep breath, looked at her husband and said in a calm voice, 'That is it! I'm taking Joey to my mother's. The marriage is over!'

She rushed upstairs to pack followed by her husband protesting at her reaction, before he started pleading with her to stay.

Joey, hiding behind the Cornish Palm in the garden saw and overheard everything. He was wondering what to do, when the house went silent.

Mummy and Daddy would be doing that soppy kissing and making-up, he reckoned, running to play on the swing.

Joey was swinging higher than he had ever done before, when he saw the magpie land in the garden. He slowed the swing down by letting his feet drag on the ground, his mind racing ten to the dozen.

Magpie, one for sorrow. Magpies liked shiny things. Mummy's wedding ring was shiny. One for sorrow! Joey ran into the house.

Disturbed by Joey, the magpie flew and perched on the garden gate, flicked its tail and gave a teasing call.

Joey ran back into the garden clutching the pistol. He steadied himself, aimed and fired at the magpie. The recoil of the pistol knocked Joey to the ground. The magpie screeched and flew away.

The bedroom window was thrown open. Bill and Jean shouted in unison.

'Joey put the gun down. It's dangerous!'

The magpie found a safe place to perch and looked down at the woman lying on the ground.

'One for sorrow,' Mavis moaned. She was as white as a ghost, and clutching a bleeding wound in her leg.

'I'm going to miss work for the first time tomorrow,' Mavis groaned, and passed out.

Hitchhiker

His worldly possessions
landed on the back seat
of my car before it stopped.
'London!' he commanded.

I didn't say, 'No', but I did say:
'No, I don't have any cigarettes,'
'No, I don't have a light,' and 'No,
I don't have anything to eat.'

I resumed my journey up the A30,
while he talked me around
European raves, Chinese opium dens,
Indian meditation and Russian orgies.

'Cornwall is a boring place,
nothing is happening here.'
He needed action. Meanwhile
it was time to chill out.

The hitchhiker didn't notice
Brown Willy or Rough Tor,
the absence of traffic noise,
grazing ponies or sheep.

He was still chilling out, mentally,
when a sudden ice-cold draught
from the opened passenger door
chilled him back in again, physically.

'Why have we stopped?'
'I'm home on Bodmin Moor.'
'You're changing! Who are you?'
'Around here they call me...

The Beast.'

THE
WITHERED
TREE

The Withered Tree

Adam Penaluna knew that there was only one Eden, and it wasn't the Cornish tourist attraction. He alluded to the original garden of Eden referred to in the Book of Genesis. However, Adam was convinced there was more than one tree of knowledge.

For as long as he could remember, forty year old Adam had this recurring dream of finding a withered tree, picking the fruit from it, and biting into it. This one act turned the dream into a memorable, mystical experience. Adam would see psychedelic colours, hear soothing music, smell fragrance of bliss, taste erotica, and touch tomorrow before it dawned.

Convinced there was a tree of knowledge in Cornwall, Adam began his search. He was very systematic. Over a period of five years he had almost covered the whole of Kerrier district. He was exploring Duvale Valley on the outskirts of Redruth, when his walking-stick suddenly took on a life of its own. The walking-stick started to act like a divining rod, jerking and twisting in Adam's hand, until it pointed to a mass of brambles growing in a dark enclosure at the bottom of the valley.

Even with the forceful pull of the walking-stick, it took Adam almost ten minutes to reach the spot. He was confronted by a wilderness convergence. Brambles twisted and weaved around each other, and grew to an incredible height. The natural, thick, and thorn-protected barrier looked like it couldn't be infiltrated. The walking-stick suddenly jerked forward. Adam had sense enough to let go before the walking-stick pulled him into the dense, prickly mass. He watched in amazement, as the walking-stick penetrated the bramble jungle until it became lost from sight.

Adam Penaluna instinctively knew that when he found the walking-stick again, he would find the tree of knowledge. He made his way slowly back up the valley. When he was almost at the top he looked back at the jungle of brambles. For the first time, the Cornishman realised something was growing out of the nucleus of bramble.

It was a tree! Adam looked again, this time through his binoculars. The tree was higher than the brambles. Its branches looked withered, as if they had almost given up the struggle for light. Adam was sure the tree was alive. He would get every form of clearance-tool, hooks, scythes, saws, and clear a path to reach the tree. By now he was positive this tree was the tree of knowledge.

The task of clearing a path to reach the tree would be one of immense physical labour. The stems of the many types of bramble intertwined. Some of the stems were as thick as a man's wrist. Many of these towered over Adam's head, then arched to touch the ground, and rooted to produce more of their prickly kind. Each of the species had differently coloured and shaped leaves. They also had their own pattern of thorns, many of which were extremely long, and razor sharp.

Arriving early the next day with an assortment of tools, Adam put on a thick pair of gardening gloves and a pair of goggles to protect his eyes. He decided to make a start by getting rid of the smaller brambles at the edge of the thorny forest with the scythe. He used low, sweeping strokes and soon cleared a fairly wide area, then decided it was time to rake away the cut stems. Adam exchanged his scythe for a long-handled rake, and dropped the front end of the rake into the cut brambles and pulled.

One of the newly-rooted arched stems appeared to be cut, but was still attached to its parent body. The stem whip-lashed and struck Adam in the face. The cutting thorns dug into his exposed flesh, and the stem wrapped itself around his body, clinging to his clothing with barbed tentacles.

Blood trickled down his forehead, under his goggles and into one eye. He slowly bent down and gasped with pain, the slight movement causing the bramble to drag razor-edged thorns across his cheeks. Eventually, he managed to pick up a small pair of hand clippers, and as carefully as possible, he snipped away small sections of the grasping stem until he had freed himself.

The Cornishman decided to lick his wounds and come back better prepared. He felt like a Celtic explorer, and made his way back to his pick-up truck, and drove home to reconsider how to clear the path to the tree.

That night, Adam had another dream about the withered tree. He was about to pick the fruit, when hundreds of brambles shot out of the ground, and wove their stems around his body. Not only were the cruel thorns cutting into his now naked body, but the brambles seemed to have a life of their own, and were behaving like a boa-constrictor with its prey. Adam was in agony. It felt as if his ribs were being crushed, and that the very breath of life was being squeezed out of him. He woke up screaming, to find himself tangled in the bed sheets.

Knowing that he had to reach the tree, Adam planned his attack on the brambles with military precision. He purchased a pair of clippers with extendable handles. He started clearing a path on the very same day. His plan was simple, and, he believed, foolproof. With the handles of the clippers extended, he cut through each bramble stem in several different places, a short distance apart. This meant only small sections of the angular thorny stem had to be raked. He raked and cleared the path in a regular pattern, putting the stems in a pile to burn them. When he lit the fire, the flames leapt skywards, and the brambles seemed to let out a scream of agony. Although it would take longer than previously anticipated, the hard-working Cornishman believed he would eventually reach the tree without harming himself further.

Adam's dreams changed on a nightly basis, all linked to the clearance work he was doing to reach the tree of knowledge. None of the dreams was of a mystical nature. Every dream varied, but they all, in some way, featured the brambles retaliating. Brambles would trip him up, and he would fall head-first into a clump of them; or he would be proceeding down the path he had cleared between the brambles, when they would suddenly shoot out of the ground, and grow to a vast height behind him, trapping him behind a wall of thorns. The only way the dreams ended was with the dreamer screaming himself awake.

On a daily basis, Adam encountered new problems with his path-making, although he had made the path over ten feet wide. On some days, he would find it blocked by long brambles from further back in the mass, crossing the path and trying to root their tips in the ground to form new shoots. Again, he would cut through them and burn the cuttings. On another occasion, he found the path blocked by new brambles shooting up from the cleared ground. Since then, every night he saturated the cleared space with a strong weed-killer, specially formulated to destroy stubborn roots.

On his twenty-third day of path-making through the natural obstacle, Adam Penaluna's path reached the tree. He spent the rest of the day clearing a circular area around the base of the tree. This was the easiest part to clear, and he realised none of the brambles actually touched or weaved themselves around the tree. The only thing touching the tree was Adam's walking-stick, no longer in its former, pristine condition. The walking-stick was now burnt black, and crumbled at his touch.

It was getting dark. Adam, exhausted by his efforts, decided to examine the tree in the light of the following day. He touched the trunk of the tree with affection. Beneath the bark, the tree was pulsating with life.

At that moment, the skies darkened, thunder roared, and lightning flashed overhead. Adam ran back down the path he had spent days making, the downpour of heavy rain soaking him to the skin. Long brambles, which were behind the trimmed brambles forming the walls of the path, lashed out and whipped at the fleeing figure with stinging accuracy. Once, the Cornishman stumbled and fell. A thin bramble that felt like barbed-wire wrapped around his throat. The sharp thorns bit into his neck. Adam snatched a small pair of clippers from his belt-holster, and managed to cut the strangling vine in several places. As soon as he was free, Adam sprang to his feet and ran as fast as the conditions allowed, until he was outside the vicious plantation.

The rain stopped as suddenly as it had started, and the dark clouds cleared. In the gathering dusk, Adam looked towards the tree of knowledge. It seemed to radiate a special energy of its own.

Adam hurried back to his transport and drove home. That night, he had a peaceful sleep without any dreams. Next morning after a hearty breakfast, he made his way back to the Duvale Valley. Adam expected to be attacked by the brambles again when he made his way to the tree. However, his journey was without incident. The brambles were limp, and dank. Life was draining out of them. It was hard to imagine the way they had previously attacked him.

He walked cautiously to the tree. It was no longer withered. Life radiated from it. Adam gazed in wonderment. This was the tree of knowledge, and it bore one single fruit - a rosy red apple!

Adam stretched out his arm to pick the solitary apple. It felt as if he were extending himself beyond consciousness, travelling through an unknown frontier, to reach the very beginning of time; right back to one incident that changed everything, until, eventually, across the centuries, it led to human life as it is in the present. Adam plucked the apple, and held it in the palm of his hand, wondering if Eve had felt as he was feeling now.

Adam polished the apple with his shirt sleeve. He smelt its fresh fragrance, and admired the beauty of the fruit resting on his open palm. This was the moment of truth. Lifting the apple to his mouth, Adam bit into it. The apple tasted divine. It was crunchy and delectably juicy in his mouth. He savoured the taste, in the same way a wine connoisseur savours an old wine.

The palatable moment was destroyed. Adam felt something slimy and wriggling in his mouth. He instinctively spat it out. From the apple-pulp that Adam spat onto the ground, a small worm-like creature wriggled into sight.

The tiny creature had landed between his feet. Adam's stomach heaved. He wanted to be sick. He also wanted to run, but was rooted to the spot.

The worm-like creature grew quickly. It had black, shiny scales, with a yellow 'V' on the front of its head. The creature did not have any eyelids. Its eyes were covered by a single transparent scale that glowed with golden light. Adam realised it was a snake, and this snake, like all snakes, was perceptive to movement; and although Adam couldn't run, he was shaking with fear, and the ominous creature was aware of his presence. The reptile used the powerful muscles of its underside to raise itself up. By now, the snake was as tall as the Cornishman. The forked tongue flicking in and out sampled the air, and tasted fear. Adam heard a faint click, as the snake dislocated its lower jaw from the other bones in its skull. The snake's skin stretched like elastic. Adam saw the gape of its mouth open wide. The head of the reptile was level with his face, saliva dripping from the fangs in its mouth.

Adam screamed. The gigantic viper reared above his head, and slowly drew the fore-part of its body into an S-shaped loop. At precisely the right moment, the gaping mouth opened wider and wider. The snake lowered itself with lightning speed to encircle the human head. The screams became fainter. Adam was lifted up and swallowed head-first. His body jerked and twisted as it passed beyond the snake's throat, and into its digestive tract with relative ease. Nothing of Adam Penaluna's body remained outside of the snake, although the contours of the Cornishman's body changed the shape of the snake, as it slowly digested the meal it had been waiting for, after centuries of hibernation since its first appearance in the Garden of Eden.

Winter Harvest

Almost all that remains of the wall built in the reign of
Henry VIII around the Cornish town of Launceston, is
Southgate, which spans the main street. This was once one
of the entrance gates to Launceston, and, some say,
the entrance to Cornwall itself. The historical facts of the
grand Southgate did not interest Dingo Pepper. He slunk
into the shadows of the pavement passage under Southgate
arch. His cynically pessimistic mood blended with the
deepening darkness of the winter afternoon.

The inner knot of tension that had gripped Dingo
Pepper like a vice when he stepped out of his car, eased.
The aura from the former debtors' prison above the
Southgate arch was vaguely familiar. It emphasised
Dingo's need for money, and provided the conviction
needed.

Dingo peered out. He saw the fat figure of Charlie
Walton waddle out of Race Hill Bookmakers' to make his
customary visit to the Cornwall Bank in Southgate Street.
Dingo Pepper exposed his canine teeth in what passed for a
smile.

Charlie Walton was blissfully unaware he was the
subject of Dingo Pepper's attention. In fact he had never
seen or heard of the lurking figure. The Launceston bookie
was gloating. His betting shop had made a profit of over
£6,000 this week. Only £1,000 of this would go through
the accounts of his business. The rest of the money, Charlie
had in his briefcase to lodge in his safety-deposit box at the
Cornwall Bank. Later, he would move it by dubious means
to an offshore account.

'Bloody bookies,' Dingo Pepper muttered, hugging
the threadbare coat to his wiry frame. The gun in its

shoulder holster bulged more solidly than muscle ever could.

Pale blue cigar smoke, filtered by deep inhaling, drifted through Charlie Walton's obese lips as he approached the Southgate arch. Dingo Pepper smelt the aroma and eased the gun out of its shoulder holster.

Charlie Walton saw the glint of metal as Dingo Pepper moved out of the gloom. The cliché, 'don't approach this man, he is armed and dangerous,' flashed through the bookie's mind. He turned with amazing agility for such a fat man. It was not quick enough. The pistol was already against his ribs. 'Walk over to the white Ford parked across the street, and get in the car by the passenger door,' Dingo hissed.

Charlie Walton was no hero. He felt a sudden need for the toilet. With the embarrassment and discomfort of a wet crotch, he did exactly what the gunman requested. Dingo Pepper got into the car driving seat and Charlie babbled his first words.

'Take the briefcase, it's full of money. I won't say anything. Honest!' Charlie Walton crossed his heart with his free hand and then undid the briefcase safety chain from around his wrist.

Dingo Pepper smirked, revealing the pointed edges of his teeth. 'Undo the combination locks and put the case on the back seat.' He prodded the bookie in the ribs with the barrel of the gun.

Beads of sweat stood out on Charlie Walton's face. His podgy fingers fumbled with the combination locks and the briefcase clicked open.

'There's over six grand here.' Charlie turned and pushed the unlocked briefcase through the gap between the front seats of the car. The fat man struggled, but managed to lift the case of money onto the back seat of the car. Thinking it was time to go, Charlie went to open the passenger door. The pistol jabbed his ribs again.

'Not yet, we are going for a little drive,' Dingo growled. He felt in control of the situation, and smirked.

The canine teeth and staring eyes of the unknown perpetrator, unnerved Charlie. The bookie's bladder emptied of its own free will for the second time that day.

'Good job this isn't my car,' Dingo snapped. He slipped the gun back into its holster, turned the starting key and accelerated into the traffic. He drove through the town and out the other side, then turned off into a housing estate and stopped the car near a police station.

'It's always safer to do things near a police station,' Dingo explained, taking the pistol out of its holster and pointing it at his passenger's head. He continued, 'I'm going to walk around to your side of the car and open the door. You will get out, open the back door of the car, then put all the money into this holdall and hand me the holdall. Do you understand?'

Charlie nodded. Dingo nipped immediately around the car and opened the passenger door. The gun menacingly waved the bookie out of the car. Charlie closed the front car door and opened the back car door quickly. He bent forward and scrabbled the bundles of notes out of the briefcase, and into the holdall. He straightened up and handed the bag full of money to the watchful gunman.

'Can I go now?' Charlie whimpered.

Dingo sneered and displayed the canine teeth that earned him his nickname. 'Guess what? We're going for another drive. Walk to the red Austin parked in front of us. Open the passenger door and get inside.'

Charlie did as he was bid. When Dingo started the Austin, he did a three-point turn and headed the car towards the A30 road, and the heart of Cornwall.

Dingo pushed the car up to eighty miles an hour, until he was forced to slow down because of patches of thick fog. When they reached Five Lanes, Dingo turned the car off the main road and drove towards Altarnun. He stopped outside the Cathedral of the Moor.

Dingo wasn't a church lover and wouldn't have appreciated the splendour of the building, dedicated to St Non, even if it were not obscured by the swirling mist.

Charlie Walton was ordered out of the car at gun-point. He started to protest. Dingo snarled and cocked the pistol. The fat man heaved himself out of the car passenger seat and stumbled into the church yard.

'That's far enough,' Dingo hissed. He put the pistol to the bookie's ear and pulled the trigger. The fat man's bowels opened, and blood, carrying fragments of bone, gushed from the gaping bullet hole as Charlie Walton crumpled into a heap at his killer's feet.

The stench from the corpse and the copper odour of blood made Dingo urge. He deposited his fish-and-chip lunch over a headstone, without a single thought of respect for the delicately carved design, carved by a young Neville Northey Burnard.

Dingo went back to the car and got into the driving seat. He opened a small panel on the dashboard, took out a flask of whiskey, raised it to his lips, and took a large swig. He wiped his mouth with his hand and replaced the flask of whiskey.

Dingo cursed the mist that was getting thicker, and drove out of the village back onto the main A30 road, and headed south.

The car was crawling along at a speed that didn't exceed ten miles an hour. The killing of the Launceston bookie seemed a life-time ago. Dingo had the window down and was driving with his head stuck out of the window opening trying to get better vision. It was impossible. Mist clung to the car like a shroud.

The car went over several bumps. Dingo braked. The car stopped, and he applied the handbrake and got out of the car. He left the car lights on and the engine running. Dingo walked around the dark shape of the car, felt underneath and around all of its wheel areas, and realised he had driven off the road onto moorland.

Dingo cursed, 'Bloody fog, bloody countryside!'

He stood up and looked around helplessly. He dare not drive any further, and he dare not leave the car. Dingo Pepper smoked only on the odd occasion. This seemed like an appropriate time. He opened a packet of Capstan full-strength, put a cigarette into his mouth, struck a match to light the cigarette and inhaled the full strength deeply. At first he thought it must be a reflection of the burning cigarette end, but every so often a yellow glow seemed to appear in the distance. Dingo inhaled again before dropping the cigarette and stubbing it out with his shoe. The mist seemed to shift in the distance, and he was sure he could see a light. The killer edged carefully forward, and every step he took, he moved his forward foot to the left and to the right, feeling the ground. Another step, and he felt the ground harden. He bent down and touched the surface.

Tarmac! Dingo turned and looked back. The light from the headlights could be seen. The mist was lifting. Dingo Pepper retraced his steps to the car, opened the driver's door and got in. He turned the lights off, and waited.

Within minutes he saw the light in the distance more clearly. After a quarter of an hour, Dingo could make out the shape of a building with two lights shining from downstairs windows. He put the car into first gear, turned the lights on and edged forward. The wind-screen wipers kept the window free of the damp mist, and through the arcing wiper-blade Dingo could see he was getting closer to the lights.

* * * * *

The Harvester was once a 13th century thatched cottage on the wagon trail running from Roughtor, across the spine of the moor, and down to Fowey. The isolated cottage became the haunt of highwaymen and smugglers in the 15th century. The low-beamed-ceiling parlour was used as a meeting place for moorland dwellers and farmers, who eked a living from the harsh landscape. They called it the Kiddley Wink, and if they wanted a drop of smuggled brandy, they would wink at the kettle in the corner. Slowly, the cottage became an inn that kept its character, but changed its name to The Harvester in the 19th century.

The Harvester still had a thatched roof. The cob wall between the kitchen and parlour was knocked down to make the present-day low-beamed-ceiling bar. Cheery warmth was provided by an open log fire, and an olde worlde atmosphere was enhanced by the hooks, sickles, scythes, pitch forks and fading photographs of horse-drawn hay-wagons that decorated the walls.

The last sheaf of corn cut at nearby Tor Farm for the yearly end-of-harvest ceremony, 'Crying the Neck', was always displayed behind the bar of the pub on the moor until it was replaced with the next year's last-cut sheaf of corn.

* * * * *

The Harvester had been in the Treloar family for generations. Bessie Treloar, the current landlady, was the last of the Treloars. She had never married. However, Bessie had enjoyed the company of many of the local farmers over the years, and despite numerous attempts by one and all, including the highly fertile, she failed to get pregnant. Bessie always said she would keep trying with any man that came from good Cornish stock.

At forty-five, Bessie was very attractive. Her plump figure with its ample bosom was most becoming. Her long, jet-black curly hair high-lighted sparkling eyes, and an ever-ready smile that dimpled round rosy cheeks.

Bessie sat in an old armchair enjoying her customary smoke from a clay pipe. She always said it was one of the best times of the day - a touch pipe with a drink of cider before the customers arrived, in front of a fire that inspired day dreams.

Dingo Pepper slowly and quietly opened the front door of The Harvester. He slipped inside and surveyed the bar. It appeared empty. Dingo wiped his lips on the sleeve of his coat, drew his lips back, and sniffed the public house aroma.

'Anybody home?' Dingo asked loudly. Turning to a sound of movement coming from the far side of the room, he exposed his canine teeth in a forced smile.

Bessie stood up, placed her clay pipe into an ash tray, and frowned with disappointment before she put on her greeting-the-visitor look.

'Come in me 'ansum,' she said in a welcoming Cornish accent. 'What would you like to drink?'

'Pint o' bitter.'

Bessie went behind the bar and took down a beer mug. She bent down, and filled the mug with a pint of bitter straight from a large wooden barrel resting on a strong shelf built about a foot above the floor. Dingo stared at the curve of Bessie's buttocks through her long, black, clinging skirt.

'Looks good,' Dingo hissed, as Bessie put the pint on the bar. 'What? My bottom, or the beer?'

Dingo exposed his pointed teeth in what passed for a smile. 'Both, now you mention it. How much?'

'One 'n' fourpence for the beer, if you please. The other is not for sale,' Bessie replied with good humour in her voice.

Dingo sorted through his loose change and put the right money on the bar.

'Got any grub?' he asked abruptly.

'Would you like a 'ome-made pasty? 'Tes still warm.'

'Sounds good,' Dingo nodded and displayed his canine teeth. 'What about a room?' He picked up the holdall. 'I wanted to make Falmouth, but I won't in this mist.'

'No rooms, but you can sleep in the armchair if that's any help, and I'll just charge you for breakfast in the morning.'

Dingo nodded, 'It'll be warmer than the car.'

' 'Tes sorted, then,' Bessie said. 'I'll go 'n' get you your pasty.' She entered the kitchen behind the bar and came back with a pasty that hung over the side of the dinner plate.

'Christ!' Dingo exclaimed. 'that's one hell-of-a pasty.'

Bessie smiled. 'I'll only charge you a shilling for it. You can pay for the food when you settle up in the morning. Just pay for the drinks as you go. Sit over there at the table, 'tes more comfortable than trying to eat at the bar. I'll finish me smauke before the regulars come in.' She moved from behind the bar to sit in her chair by the fire.

Dingo took his pint and the pasty over to the indicated table and sat down. He took a bite from the pasty and realised the holdall was at the bar. He got up and walked across and picked it up.

'Must have the crown jewels in there, the way you are guarding that bag!' Bessie said, turning to look at Dingo.

'No, no, just like to keep me stuff safe,' Dingo said with a snarl, then realised he was the only customer. He saw Bessie looking at him. He gave a hard, forced smile. 'Force of habit. London you know.'

Bessie smiled, put a taper in the fire, took it out again, sat back, and lit her clay pipe and inhaled the essence of deep rich tobacco.

* * * * *

Dingo pushed away his empty plate and moved towards the bar. He turned to Bessie, who rose from her chair in front of the fire and made her way behind the bar.

'Nothing like a bit of home-made grub. I'll round it off with a drop of whiskey,' Dingo smirked and continued, 'Tell you what, make it a double. I'm having a good day...'

Bessie poured a generous double whiskey and placed it in front of her only customer. 'Cash or Harvest?' she asked, and quickly corrected herself, 'Half-a-crown for cash.'

Dingo put a coin near his glass on the counter. Bessie bent forward to pick up the silver halfcrown-piece. Dingo tried to sneak a look at the landlady's cleavage which the low-fronted top revealed.

'Home grown,' Bessie remarked proudly, stepping back and thrusting her bust forward in a provocative manner, 'but not available.'

Dingo licked his lips. He ran his tongue around his pointed teeth. 'Everything is available for the right price,' he stated, and went back to sit at the table.

The front door of The Harvester opened and a tall, well-built man in his early forties entered briskly. He had a hessian sack over his shoulders to keep him dry.

' 'Ansum weather for ducks!' the newcomer exclaimed, as he hung the hessian sack on a peg behind the pub door. He wore a tough and durable Cornwall Rugby jersey tucked into a pair of corduroy trousers.

' 'Usual, Alfred?' Bessie asked, and started to draw a pint before Alfred had a chance to answer.

Alfred, who had the look of a farmer and the build of a rugby player, balanced on one leg and then the other as he pulled off his Wellington Boots. He walked to the bar in a pair of home-knitted socks. 'One of these nights, I might demand something different, Bessie Treloar, and make you throw the pint you've poured, down the drain.'

Bessie smiled, 'Cash or Harvest, Alfred?' she inquired. 'Harvest, maid, - you know that by now. I'm only a poor farmer, struggling to survive the elements Bodmin Moor throws at me.'

Alfred took a long sip at his drink. He turned and looked at Dingo. 'Your health, sire!'

Dingo nodded and curled his lip back to reveal the points of his teeth.

'Time for introductions. This is Alfred. He owns Tor Farm. I'm Bessie and you're...?'

Dingo scowled. 'Smith, Mr Smith.'

At that moment, the front door of The Harvester burst open, and a female in her early twenties rushed through the door. She bent forward and shook her head. Water sprayed from her hair.

'God!' she exclaimed, 'it suddenly pissed down!'

'Doc!' Bessie protested loudly.

'Ah! I'm bloody soaked,' the girl said, and looked up. 'Sorry!' She gaped open-mouthed at Dingo. 'I never realised we had company.' Her face lit up. She smiled, and walked towards Dingo holding out her hand in a greeting of friendship. 'Sorry about that. I'm Angela... They call me Doc...' She paused, her hand still out-stretched. She lowered it, slowly. 'And you're...?'

'This is Mr Smith!' Bessie intervened.

'Alright,' Dingo said abruptly. He looked at the girl referred to as Doc, undressing her with his eyes as he looked her up and down, before his look lingered on the wet shirt clinging to her shapely breasts. 'Another double whiskey landlady,' Dingo demanded as he turned and walked towards the bar.

The other two customers looked at each other and raised their eyebrows.

Bessie placed the ordered drink in front of Dingo.

'Half-a-crown please, Mr Smith,' Bessie said politely. Dingo put a coin on the bar and moved slowly in the direction of the open fireplace.

'What would you like, Doc?' Bessie asked the pretty, but bedraggled, young girl, as she handed her a towel to dry herself.

'I'll have a drop of whiskey,' Doc answered as she rubbed her hair with the towel. 'I don't want to catch a cold. A vet with a cold is no good to man or beast.'

'Cash or Harvest Doc?' Bessie asked placing the ordered drink on the bar.

'Harvest, I'm skint till the end of the month.'

'What's all this cash or harvest?' Dingo asked with a scowl as he moved back towards the bar. 'Am I the only one paying in cash?' he said menacingly, and asked sharply, 'Is harvest some kind of country bumpkin tick, like a slate is up north?'

Alfred laughed loudly, and the two females smiled.

'It's right the reverse, my 'ansum,' Alfred said, and chuckled before he continued, 'we don't go into debt around here. Harvest is money we've already got behind the bar!'

Bessie nodded. 'As landlady, I can honestly say, harvest is money everyone here has got put back to see us through the lean times.'

'How much you got put back then?' Dingo inquired innocently, and looked away so they couldn't detect the look of interest in his eyes.

'That's only for us to know!' Doc said in a firm, quiet voice, 'and Bessie, I'll have another whiskey on the strength of a good harvest.'

'And I'll have another pint,' Alfred said, and laughed. His large shoulders shook with mirth.

'I'll join you.' Bessie put the two ordered drinks on the bar and poured herself a large whiskey.

The three locals raised their glasses. 'Harvest!' they said in unison, and all laughed.

'Come on!' Dingo exclaimed. 'Come on, you can't leave me in suspense.'

Bessie, Alfred and Doc looked at one another and smiled. The silence was broken by a clock chiming out the half hour somewhere in a room behind the bar.

'Time!' said Bessie.

'Time!' exclaimed Dingo tensely. 'It's only half past seven!'

'Time!' Bessie repeated more loudly. 'Time... to tell you about Harvest.'

Dingo relaxed his wiry frame as he realised he had been had. He tried to smile, but the face he pulled looked more like a dog snarling, and it made Alfred chuckle again.

'I'll tell you what Harvest is,' Alfred said when he had regained his composure. 'Every summer we get hundreds of visitors here, who all want to know about life on the moor. They all buy us more drink than we can ever drink in one session. Bessie keeps tally, and at the end of the season we have a harvest of plenty to keep us watered through the long winter.'

Dingo looked in amazement and said with awe in his voice, 'You canny lot of buggers.' He put his hand in his pocket and put two five pound notes on the bar. 'Put that in your funds and tell me about life on the moor.'

Dingo's eyes never left the five pound notes, and his disappointment was plain to see when Bessie scooped them up and placed them down her top in the care of her ample bosoms.

'Well ...' said Doc, 'cheers, first of all. One of the many things I get asked is, why everyone calls me Doc. Most assume it is because I'm the local vet, but I've been called Doc, since I was ten years old. Whenever I found an injured creature, I always tried to help it. Even down to putting sticky tape on broken snail shells.'

'That's true. I remember,' Alfred said with a chuckle, 'you even tried to revive a dead goldfish with the kiss of life!'

'For that,' interrupted Doc, 'I've got to tell Mr Smith about the night you slept with the ghosts that haunt that ramshackle old farm house you call home!'

'You mean, the night I slept with the goats!' exclaimed Alfred, who chuckled again.

'Hang on a minute!' Dingo said, 'I've got to have a slash'

'Through the door, turn right ...' Bessie informed Dingo who was looking everywhere but the right direction.

Dingo went to pick up his holdall. He hesitated, picked up the holdall, and headed for the door Bessie had indicated.

'I'll have a quick wash while I'm out there,' Dingo said by way of explanation for taking the holdall with him, as he went through the door that led to the convenience.

'Funny chap,' said Bessie quietly.

'What do you reckon ...?'

Before Alfred could finish what he was going to say, the pub front door opened and a young, good-looking policeman hurried in.

'Bobby! Bobby!' Doc exclaimed, and ran over and put her arms around the young policeman and kissed him passionately.

Bobby, the local policeman, gently pushed away the attractive girl who his fiancée.

'Doc, I'm on duty... Bessie, Alfred ... whose car is that outside?'

'Some up-the-country fella - got lost and is sheltering from the weather for the night... I think he's heading for Falmouth.'

'Where is he!' Bobby asked with an intense urgency in his voice.

Bessie.pointed towards the toilets. The policeman breathed in and took out his truncheon.

'Leave this to me,' Bobby stated and moved towards the toilet door.

Dingo entered with a gun in one hand and his holdall in the other. He pointed his gun at the young policeman. 'Back off, copper!' Dingo snarled, and edged into the room. 'All of you - back against the bar!' Dingo indicated with the gun.

'Put the gun down, you fool!' Bobby said, and bravely stepped towards Dingo.

'I'm arresting you on suspicion of murder...!'

Doc screamed, 'No! Bobby, stay back!'

Dingo was distracted. The four locals all seemed to move at the same time. He tried to cover them all. Bessie ducked down behind the bar. Doc staggered from the push Bobby gave her, before he tried to grab Dingo's gun arm with his free hand.

In the commotion, Alfred dived to the nearest wall and snatched down a scythe. Dingo stepped aside to avoid

Bobby's wildly swinging truncheon, and in the very same moment, Alfred made a low sweep with the scythe.

Dingo screamed like a tortured animal. The long sharp blade cut through his trousers into the backs of his legs, slicing into his calves. The merciless scythe ripped through the muscles, and cracked shin bones, before glancing off and tearing a strip of flesh into a flap, that hung with torn muscles. Blood from the hideous wound sprayed everywhere. Dingo's lean body was like a toppled tree, and he started to fall backwards. The gun in his hand went off, firing a bullet into the ceiling.

'I 'ave 'un! I 'ave 'un! I 'ave 'un!' Alfred shouted triumphantly, above Dingo's screams of agony.

Dingo's body crashed to the floor. He was still screaming. He fired the gun again without aiming, and the bullet tore a piece out of the front of the bar. Dingo was in agony. He knew it was a fight to the death and tried to stand. Bobby, the young policeman, grabbed hold of a handful of Dingo's hair and pulled his head back. Dingo was weakening quickly from the loss of blood, and the pain. His arms flayed about aimlessly. The gun dropped from his hand and fell to the floor. Dingo howled like a cornered beast that couldn't defend itself.

Bobby yanked Dingo's head back again. The vicious killer's neck went taut. It was taut long enough for Bessie to take aim. With all of her might, she made a sweeping blow with a razor-sharp machete she had taken from behind the bar.

The one powerful blow, with a tool being used as a lethal weapon, and wielded in total defensive anger by the Harvester landlady, was enough to sever Dingo's head from his twitching body. Blood spurted from the headless corpse like a fountain, covering the four attackers who descended on the body as one.

Bobby the policeman pulled clear, dragging Dingo's detached head with him.

Alfred shouted triumphantly again 'I 'ave 'en! I 'ave 'en! I 'ave 'en!' The blood-soaked women staggered to their feet.

'What 'ave 'ee?' they asked wearily in unison.

Bobby held the severed head at arm's length.

'A neck! A neck! A neck!' they all shouted.

* * * * *

Bessie and her three regular customers worked into the night cleaning the blood-stained bar. Dingo's body and severed head had been wrapped in tarpaulin and lay on the back seat of his car, still parked outside the front door of the The Harvester, with the young policeman's bike leaning against the car door.

Bessie filled four glasses with whiskey and sat down with her exhausted customers around one of the tables.

'I need this!' Bessie raised her glass.

'Down the hatch,' Alfred replied, and emptied his glass.

'What are we going to do with the body?' Bessie asked.

Alfred stretched his arm across the table and put his hand on Bessie's hand.

'I push the car with the body in it down Bal Tor mine shaft before it gets light.'

'Will anybody ever find it?' Doc asked with a worried look on her face.

'No-one ever found the other three cars and at least six bodies I've tipped down that shaft over the years.'

'Just make sure you're not seen from the road,' the young policeman added, to voice his concern.

'How much did you find in his pockets?' Doc asked turning to look at Bobby.

'Just over twenty quid,' Bobby replied. 'I gave it to Bessie for the Harvest fund.'

'Bloody hell!' exclaimed Doc. 'We forgot about his bag.'

'I'll get it,' Alfred stated.

He walked across the room. The bag must have got pushed into a dark corner, near the toilet door, during the activity earlier. Alfred picked up the holdall and walked back to the table. He placed the holdall on his chair and undid the zip.

'Bloody hell!' Alfred exclaimed, as he pulled out wads of £5 notes.

'He must have robbed that bookie before he murdered him,' Bobby remarked in an official-sounding police voice.

'Never mind that,' said Bessie with a smile, 'this looks like the best harvest we've ever had, and to top that, it's a winter harvest!'

'I'll drink to that,' Alfred chuckled.

They all raised their glasses and clinked them with the toast,

'Winter Harvest!'

End Papers

This transcript of a recording was found when Goon Carn Research Station, North Cornwall, was raided in the interests of National Security.

Dr Livingstone-Noble:

This is the control centre of Goon Carn Research Station, Kernow, Planet Earth, broadcasting on all known wavebands in audio, all known channels on audio-visual, and universe-wide in virtual reality, and also by time-travel simulation across all aeons from the beginning of the universe. Today's date is October 27 in the year 2224. Earth time is 12.00 o'clock midnight.
If either Mitchell (artist) or Merton (writer) who are also known as Trystan Mitchell and Les Merton can hear this, please respond in anyway you can.

Mitchell:

Hello, control centre, your voice is faint but I can hear you. Are you the same Dr Livingstone-Noble from the 21st Century?

Dr Livingstone-Noble:

Yes, the very same. Death was overcome in the year 2040. Have you had any contact with Merton?

Mitchell:

Nothing since we left in October 2004, to travel forward into the future with time-travel of the mind.

Merton:

I can hear both of you, where are you Trystan?

Mitchell:

It feels like I am in a large wooden box. There is a smell of must and decay, and now I have got used to the dark, I can see reasonably well.

Merton:

Good to hear you, Trystan. I am in a similar box. It feels like a coffin, although it is tall enough for me to stand. I think I've been walking down a long dark passage forever.

Mitchell:

I know what you mean, Les. There doesn't seem to be any end to it.

Dr Livingstone-Noble:

You both must keep walking until you see a light. Do you understand?

Mitchell:

I think so.

Merton:

This seems like some twentieth century religious theory: when our life is over, we go down a dark tunnel towards a tiny light shining in the distance. Are we dead, when we reach the light you so casually mention?

Dr Livingstone-Noble:

I will never know...

Acknowledgements

I must thank Anthony Delgrado of bluechrome publishing and boho press, who on the promise of an apple at Christmas put up with my many frames of mind to see this book and it's predecessor, *As Yesterday Begins*, through to their natural conclusions.

I am extremely grateful to Trystan Mitchell for his help, friendship and for illustrating what is in my mind - sometimes before I realised it was there.

No book of mine would ever make it if I didn't have a dedicated proof reader. Sylvia Mitchell gave freely of her time and advice and I am very indebted to her.

Special thanks to all the staff of Kresenn Kernow - The Cornwall Centre for always being there when needed.

I would like to credit my cousin Brian Thomas for planting the name Dingo Pepper in my young impressionable mind. I am also indebted to Pol Hodge for many other names used in this book. These were inspired by his 'Cornish Names' dictionary.

I am obliged to small press magazines; Lookout, Chillout, Linkway for publishing earlier versions of some of the work included in this collection.

I must acknowledge Kernow for always being home to me and last but by no means least I must pay homage to the dark corners of my mind that were always there in times of need.

Dedicated

To all those helping new writers.

About Les Merton

Les Merton has been many things in his lifetime: shop manager, coal man, factory worker, film extra, door to door salesman, fortune teller, bus conductor, hotel porter, entertainment agent, failed comedian, sales director, fundraiser, publisher, editor and hopes that these days he is a writer.

His previous books are: Cornflakes and Toast, Missus Laity's Tay Room, The Spirit of a King, Light the Muse, Oall Rite Me Ansum, The Official Encyclopaedia of the Cornish Pasty, As Yesterday Begins, Adders in Cornwall.

He was made a Bard of the Gorseth Kernow (The Cornish Gorsedd) in 2004 for services to Cornish Literature and his Bardic name is Map Hallow (Son of the Moors).

About Trystan Mitchell

Trystan Mitchell has scribbled and scratched away making marks on one surface or another ever since he realised he could do more with a crayon than just chew it to a hugely satisfying gooey pulp.

Illustrator, sign-writer and writer, he has worked for several national and Westcountry publishers, appearing in The Guardian, Squall, Cornwall Today, Politics Today,'Enhancing Your Mind & Body and Spirit' and the Wooden Books series, as well as providing artwork for campaigning organisations such as Greenpeace UK and The Land Is Ours. He also does regular creative support work with the Cornwall Children's Fund and other education/welfare services in Cornwall.

Having lived as a traveller and hedge-monkey for many years, he now lives at home with himself, a slate roof, mains electric and no cats. Sometimes he gets quite animated.